the prisoner™

WARNER BOOKS

A Time Warner inc. Company

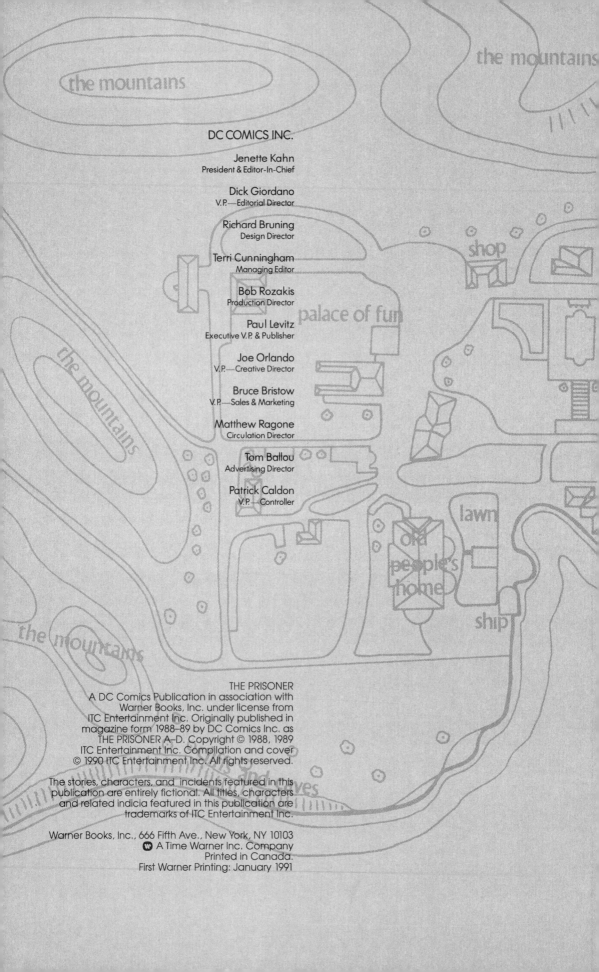

the mountains

the mountains

the mountains

the mountains

shop

palace of fun

lawn

old people's home

ship

DC COMICS INC.

Jenette Kahn
President & Editor-In-Chief

Dick Giordano
V.P.—Editorial Director

Richard Bruning
Design Director

Terri Cunningham
Managing Editor

Bob Rozakis
Production Director

Paul Levitz
Executive V.P. & Publisher

Joe Orlando
V.P.—Creative Director

Bruce Bristow
V.P.—Sales & Marketing

Matthew Ragone
Circulation Director

Tom Ballou
Advertising Director

Patrick Caldon
V.P.—Controller

THE PRISONER
A DC Comics Publication in association with
Warner Books, Inc. under license from
ITC Entertainment Inc. Originally published in
magazine form 1988–89 by DC Comics Inc. as
THE PRISONER A–D. Copyright © 1988, 1989
ITC Entertainment Inc. Compilation and cover
© 1990 ITC Entertainment Inc. All rights reserved.

Warner Books, Inc., 666 Fifth Ave., New York, NY 10103
Ⓦ A Time Warner Inc. Company
Printed in Canada.
First Warner Printing: January 1991

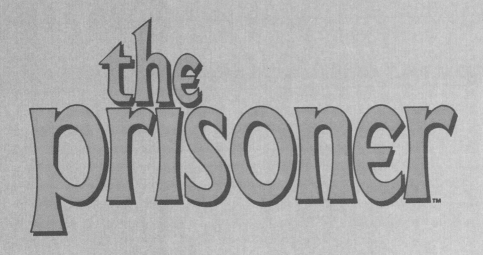

the prisoner™

shattered visage

STORY BY **dean motter**
and **mark askwith**

ILLUSTRATED BY **dean motter**

COLOR ART BY **david hornung** and **richmond lewis**

COLLECTED BOOKS
Richard Bruning & KC Carlson
Co-Editors

Richard Bruning
Editor, original series

Dean Motter
Publication Design and Cover Painting

Robert Walton
Art Assist

David Hornung (Books A, B and D)
Richmond Lewis (Book C)
Color Artists

Deborah Marks (Books A, B and C)
John Workman (Book D)
Lettering

We would like to thank
the following people
for their assistance:

Vera Litynsky
Jennifer Proud
Janis Forsey
studio assistance

Christine Partridge
and Robin Edge
computer graphics

Judith Dupré
Catherine Majoribanks
Kaveh

Very special thanks to:

Patrick McGoohan
Leo McKern
Bruce Clark
Ed Gilbert

The creative contributors
are grateful for the extensive
assistance of SIX OF ONE
The Prisoner Appreciation Society.

For further information,
Send a stamped, self-addressed
envelope to:

Six Of One
P.O. Box 172
Hatfield, PA
19440 USA

Six Of One
P.O. Box 60
Harrogate HG1 2TP
United Kingdom

the mountains

the mountains

the mountains

the mountains

shop

palace of fun

lawn

people's home

ship

cliffs and caves

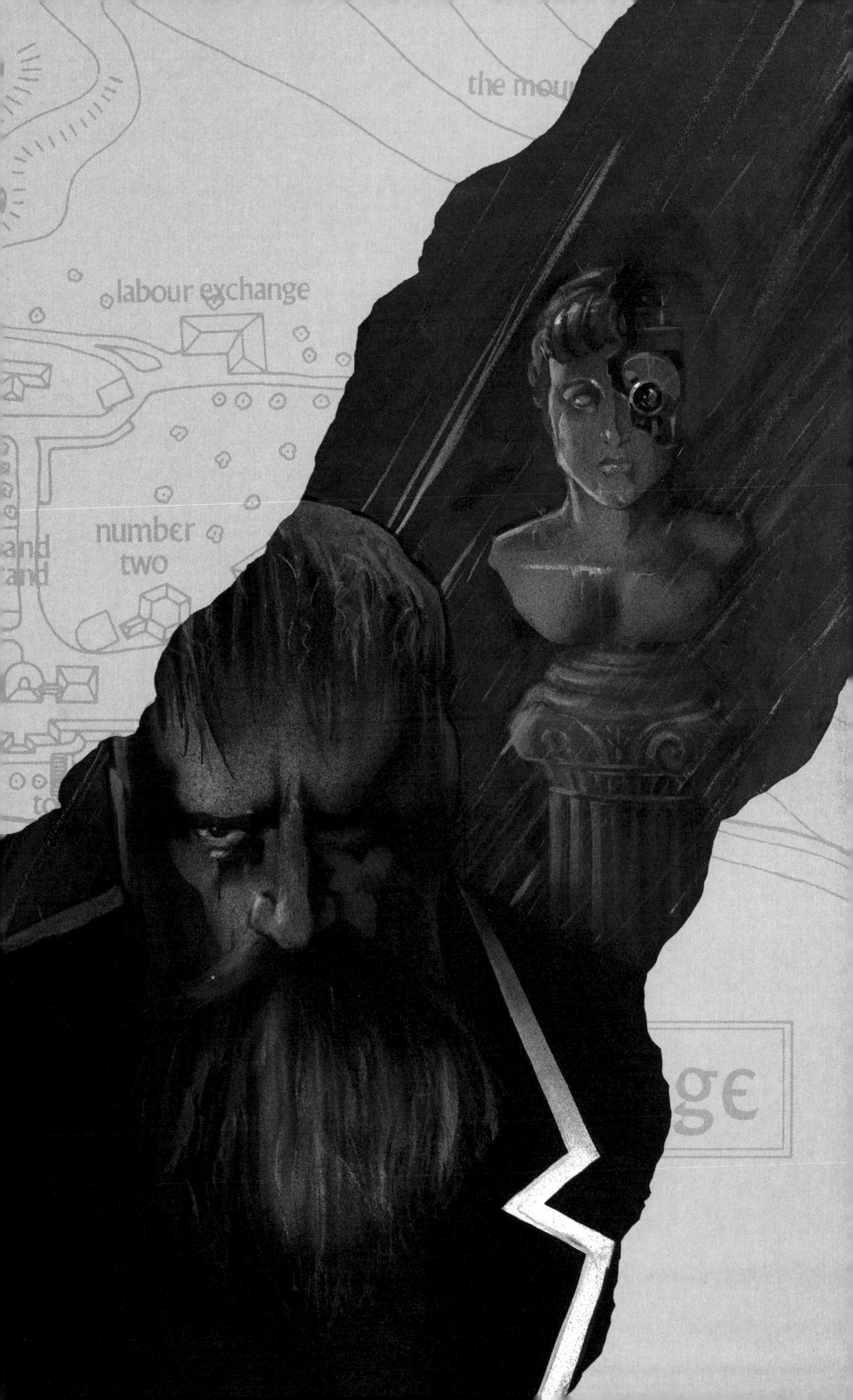
labour exchange
number two

DEAN MOTTER has worked as an illustrator/designer in animation, children's books and advertising. He served as staff illustrator at Holt, Rinehart, and Winston in Toronto for three years followed by three years as art director at CBS Records Canada.

During this time he also taught at The Ontario College Of Art and edited one of the earliest alternative genre comic books, ANDROMEDA, which boasted such authors as Arthur C. Clarke, A.E. Van Vogt, James Tiptree, and Walter M. Miller.

Dean collaborated with Ken Steacy on what is recognized as one of the first genuine graphic novels in the comic book field, THE SACRED AND THE PROFANE.

He is perhaps best known as the creator/writer of the comics sensation MISTER X, often cited as 'the designer's comic. '

His work has appeared in publications such as EPIC ILLUSTRATED, THE SPIRIT, GRENDEL and ACTION COMICS. His design work can be seen on LEGENDS OF THE DARK KNIGHT, GOTHAM BY GASLIGHT as well as several book and record covers.

Dean continues to make his living as an art director, designer, writer and illustrator in the entertainment field.

MARK ASKWITH is currently Senior Story Editor for TVOntario's PRISONERS OF GRAVITY. Mark managed Toronto's Silver Snail from 1983–87, and was the comic book advisor for the Genie Award-winning documentary film COMIC BOOK CONFIDENTIAL. His stories have appeared in TABOO, STREET MUSIC, and TRUE NORTH.

Dedicated to
Terry Anderson
and
to the memory of
Charles Hopewell English Askwith

o z y m a n d i a s

I met a traveler from an antique land
Who said: Two vast and trunkless legs of stone
Stand in the desert. Near them on the sand,
Half sunk, a shattered visage lies, whose frown
And wrinkled lip, and sneer of cold command,
Tell that its sculptor well those passions read
Which yet survive, stamped on these lifeless things,
The hand that mocked them, the heart that fed.
And on the pedestal these words appear:
"My name is Ozymandias, king of kings.
Look upon my works ye Mighty and despair!"
Nothing beside remains. Round the decay
Of that colossal wreck, boundless and bare
The lone and level sands stretch far away.

percy bysshe shelley

Code 112-112

**COMMUNIQUÉ TO
MRS. BUTTERWORTH MI-5
(Division Director-ret.)
FROM EXCAVATIONS OFFICER
DRAKE.**

**FOR YOUR EYES ONLY.
PRIVATE CODE.**

CLASSIFIED.

Following this memo is a copy of my
final report on THE VILLAGE IDIOT
manuscript revisions.

I know I shouldn't be writing this, but I feel
that you should be alerted to what I fear is an
imminent crisis. During the course of my last
assignment I made a number of discoveries
which have some rather disastrous
implications.

As my mentor I owe you a great deal, and I
would be doing you a disservice if I did not
bring the matter to your attention.

Normally I would be loathe to trouble you
with problems arising from as mundane an
action as laundering a VIP's memoirs,
however, this case has become decidedly
exceptional.

As we feared, the book hit the stands and
became a runaway bestseller. Our beloved
author will emerge from his twenty year
interment to what is certain to be a flurry of
interviews, publicity, and questions. The
media is going to want information. All kinds
of it. Especially about The Village and who
ran it.

We needn't be overly concerned, as I
managed to obfuscate the most sensitive
material in the book. *HE* will, of course,
scream cover-up. Even that can be dealt with
by other departments.

The truly dangerous topics, such as Project:
Operation Pennyfarthing, Prisoners Of
Power, Protect Other People, and Price Of
Peace have been carefully excised—as, of
course, have references to The Arch-Angels.
But it is the subject of Directive 17 that
worries me: The status of Prisoner
Number Six.

It appears that Number Six resigned from his position just over twenty years ago, and, despite the official records, not on altogether amiable terms. Details are sketchy as most of the files were destroyed. It seems he had access to a great deal of VERY sensitive information. Certainly you would know better than I, given your position in the service at the time.

From what I gather, he was detained and installed in The Village facility immediately upon his resignation.

The administration there was determined to discover exactly why he resigned, the nature and extent of his information, and ultimately what he intended to do with it.

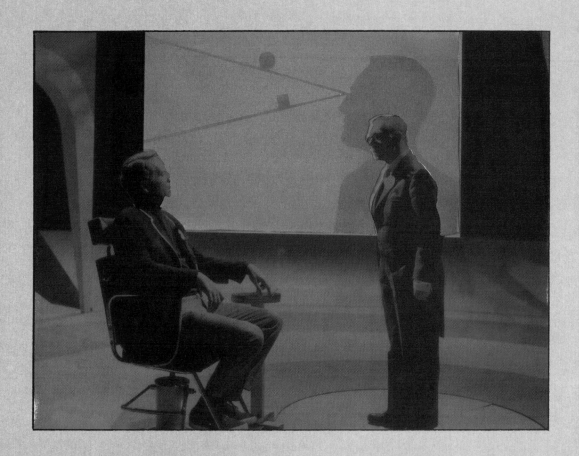

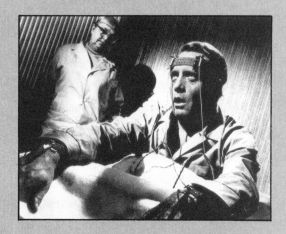

Number Six, however, proved to be highly uncooperative. He resented this treatment and a colossal struggle of wills ensued. He not only resisted his captors, but he openly defied them. The resort-like Village took on the atmosphere of a battlefield.

Number Six made several attempts to escape. The administration, in turn, interrogated him—repeatedly. And, as far as I can tell, he did not talk.

They became obsessed with Number Six. Chairman after chairman was appointed (and dismissed) specifically to break him. He was subjected to several exotic and experimental mind-control techniques.

Our dear author, the last of The Village chairmen, (or Number Two, as they were each called), engineered the most elaborate attempt of all: a theatrical tour-de-force involving actors as well as hallucinogenic drugs. He actually staged his own death and resurrection. It was positively surreal. You will find an account of it in the section of my report titled FALL OUT.

Of course, this was removed from the book as well. (Not that anyone would have believed it.)

Still, most of this is ancient history to you.

However, when the U.N. Troops liberated The Village in 1968, the Colonel's directives specified that the power to The Village's support systems *NOT* be terminated. That the food and medical provisions *NOT* be removed.

Yet The Village was evacuated.

Furthermore, the manifest of deceased and/or released inmates does not account for Number Six. Do you see what I'm leading up to?

YOU signed those manifests.

I believe that Number Six must have remained there.

Rather a good way to protect him and his information, I suppose. The location is still classified. No one has been anywhere near the place in the last two decades. And, after all, what would he come back to?

But our soon-to-be-released Number Two is going to be trouble. I know it. It can be read between every line of his manuscript. If he doesn't go to the press, he is going to go to The Village and handle the matter personally. He will undoubtedly compromise the security of Number Six (whose information, I must assume, is still extremely sensitive).

One way or another, heads will roll. Yours may well be among them. It will be a bloody inquisition.

I am petitioning for the means to stop Number Two. I need your influence—your endorsement. We are currently under severe budget restrictions but it is your personal welfare that concerns me.

Please consider this carefully.

Hope you're on your feet soon.

Thomas

B.C.N.U.

Officer Exc. 3666 Div.
In Her Majesty's Service

book

a (r)rival

6'6" MAX. HEADRO[OM]

HELLO, SIR. YOU'VE A STACK OF MESSAGES AND A FOUR O'CLOCK MEETING WITH COLONEL J.

GET D. OPS DOWN HERE STRAIGHT AWAY!

YES, SIR.

KAR 120 C

NO, SIR.

I AM WORRIED BY WHAT APPEARS TO BE A NARROWING IN SCOPE OF MY DEPARTMENT'S MANDATE. IN MY VIEW, *EXCAVATIONS*, ALWAYS A JUNIOR OFFICE, RISKS EXTINCTION IF CURRENT POLITICS PREVAIL.

YES?

REQUESTS FOR EXTRA STAFF: DENIED.

REQUESTS FOR EXTRA FUNDING: DEFERRED.

PETITION FOR SPECIAL AGENT: REJECTED.

PETITION FOR INTER-DEPARTMENTAL ASSISTANCE: DENIED.

YOUR DEPARTMENT HAS OPERATED AT CERTAIN STAFF AND BUDGET LEVELS FOR DECADES. NOW, YOUR ENTHUSIASM IS COMMENDABLE, BUT SOME MIGHT SEE YOUR REQUESTS...

...AS LITTLE MORE THAN ...EMPIRE BUILDING.

MY REQUESTS ARE LEGITIMATE, SIR. ON MONDAY, THE MAN YOU CALL *NUMBER TWO* WILL BE RELEASED FROM PRISON AFTER TWENTY YEARS. IN HIS ORIGINAL MANUSCRIPT HE MADE CERTAIN ALLEGATIONS.

I'VE TOLD YOU THAT, DESPITE OUR CONCESSIONS, HE PLANS TO AVENGE HIMSELF ON THOSE RESPONSIBLE FOR HIS INCARCERATION. ALL I WANT IS A SPECIAL AGENT TO RUN INTERFERENCE.

DO YOU REALLY THINK *NUMBER TWO* IS A THREAT? HE WAS, AFTER ALL, QUITE HANDSOMELY COMPENSATED.

YES, SIR. TO THE POINT THAT I AM PREPARED TO BACK MY CONCERN...

...WITH MY RESIGNATION.

the holiday begins.

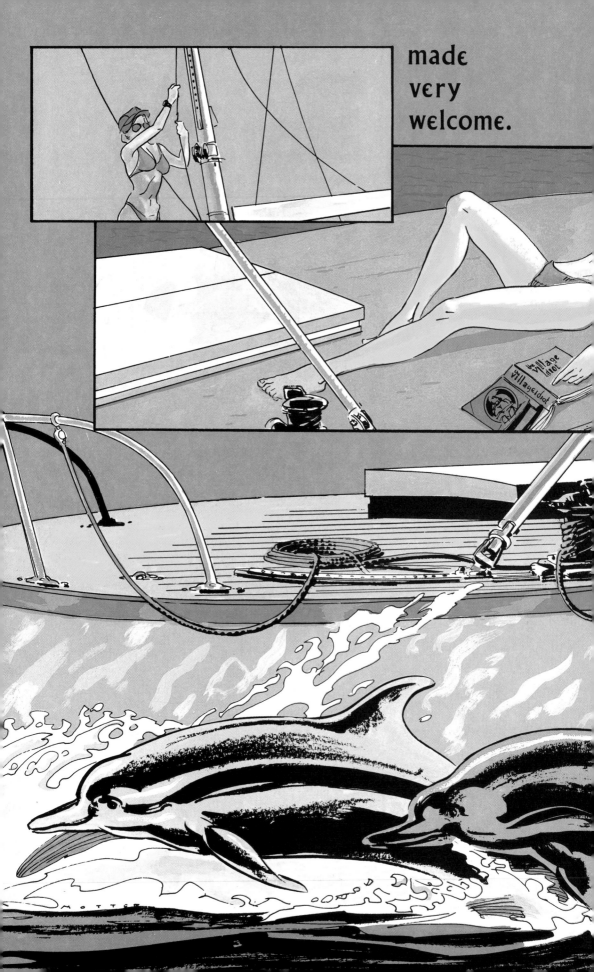

made
very
welcome.

arrived today.

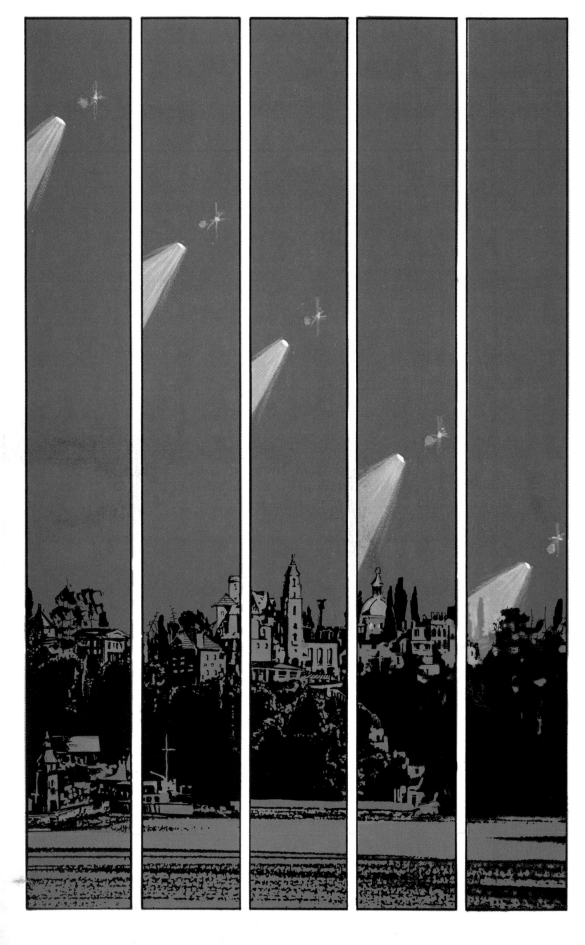

book

by hook
or by
crook

monday

TODAY ...
A BEAUTIFUL DAY

VISIT N

tuesday

ARRIVED TODAY...
—MADE VERY
WELCOME.

THE TALLY HO

on...

egins at last

map of
your
village

THE TALLY HO

vacation...

holiday begins at last

map o
your
village

RISE AND SHINE.

WERE YOU ABLE TO FIND OUT WHY LAKE WAS TAILING ME?

I DIDN'T HAVE A CHANCE TO TALK WITH HIM BEFORE HIS ACCIDENT.

AND THE GODS?

NO WORD. THEY DON'T FRATERNIZE MUCH WITH THE HELP.

WHAT CAN THEY SUSPECT ME OF...?

I WONDER HOW *SHE'S* DOING?

FINE, I SHOULD THINK. I HAVEN'T CHECKED WITH TRISH LATELY.

I HEAR SHE RAN INTO A BIT OF HEAVY WEATHER. HURRICANE JUDITH. LOST CONTACT FOR AWHILE.

I'M NOT TOO WORRIED. SHE'S A CAPABLE SAILOR AND THE ADVENTURE IS JUST TRUMPED UP FOR THE PRESS. LET'S FACE IT, ROSS. BETWEEN RADIO, COMPUTER AND THE SATELLITES, SHE'S ON A GODDAMNED GUIDED TOUR.

I'VE BEEN WONDERING ABOUT THAT MYSELF. THIS WHOLE ADVENTURE STARTED BECAUSE I FELT I HAD BOTTOMED OUT; DEPRESSED.

MY MARRIAGE, MY WORK SEEMED CLAUSTROPHOBIC.

AN ENDLESS UPHILL BATTLE.

I WAS TRAPPED. IT WAS EITHER ESCAPE, OR GET OVER IT.

I NEEDED--

AS I THOUGHT.

PREDICTABLE.

ALMOST EVERYONE PICKS THREE. SUBLIMINAL CONDITIONING. CIVILIZATION HAS BRANDED YOU. YOU'LL NEVER BE FREE UNLESS YOU VIEW EVERYONE AND EVERYTHING AS SUSPECT.

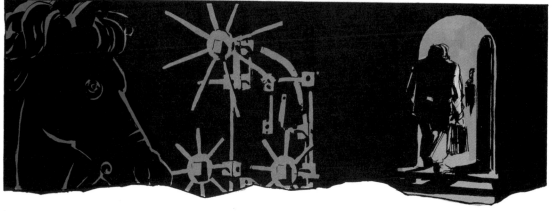

YOU'RE VERY KIND, ACTUALLY.

COOKING FRESH FISH, DELIVERING TEA THIS MORNING--

THE PERFECT HOST!

THE TEA? WASN'T MY DOING.

THEN WHO?

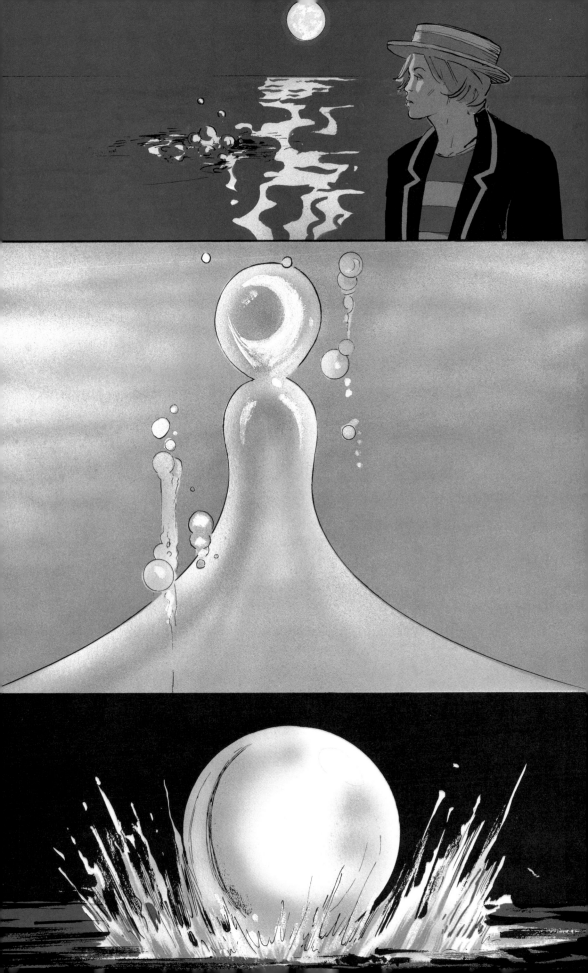

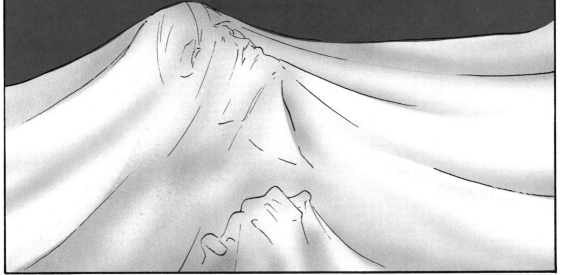

...MAROONED?

WE JUST WANTED HER TO SAIL BY THERE!

IT'S OVER, LEE.

I'M GOING TO LOSE IT ALL!

DON'T PANIC! THIS DOESN'T HAVE TO BE ANOTHER HASENFUS FIASCO! SURE THERE'LL BE A SEARCH, BUT WHILE THEY WORK OUT THEIR GAME PLAN, WE'LL WORK OUT OURS.

WE'VE GOT A LOOSE BALL, TOM. WE HAVE TO GRAB IT AND RUN WITH IT.

WHAT IF HE KILLS HER?

MORE THAN LIKELY SHE'LL KILL HIM.

SHE'S GOT HER GUN, AND HAS NO QUALMS ABOUT USING IT.

BESIDES, SHE'S A TRAINED AGENT. SHE KNOWS THE RISKS.

NO, SHE DOESN'T.

NOT THIS TIME.

WELL—

—COME.

...WELCOME...

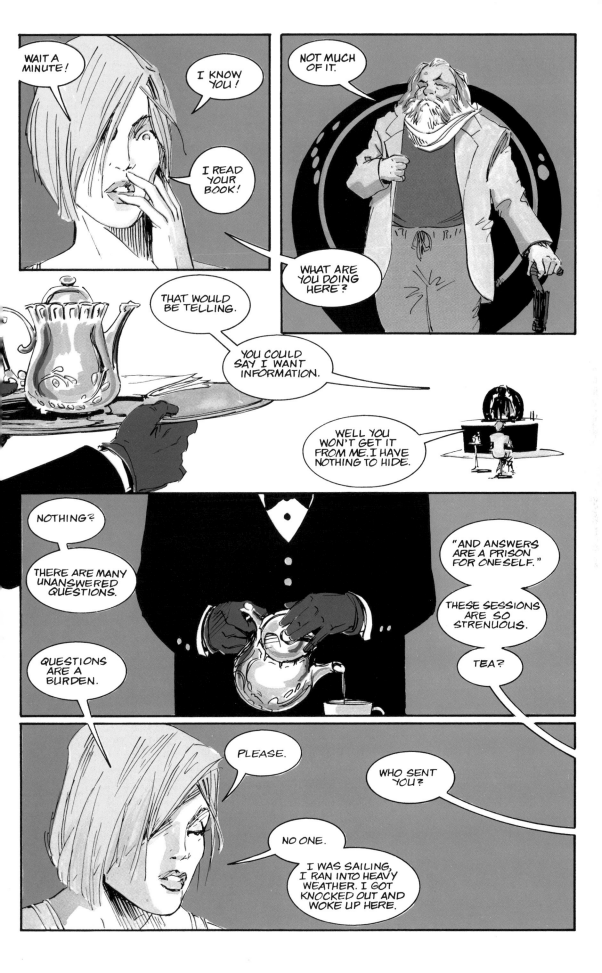

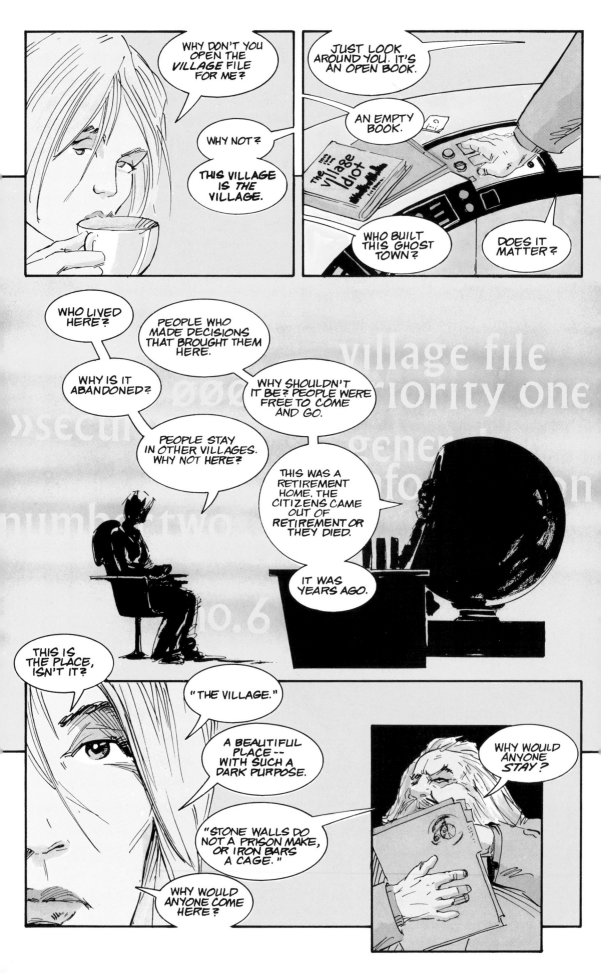

A-HA! A MAN OF MANY TALENTS; ATHLETE, SOLDIER, PILOT, STATESMAN

...AND MANY NAMES. IN FRANCE-- JACQUES DUVAL. IN GERMANY-- FRIEDRICH SCHMIDT.

IN CANADA-- JOHN WHITE. CODE NAME URIEL. CODE NUMBER ZM-73

A VALUABLE MAN, WHO KEPT VALUABLE SECRETS...

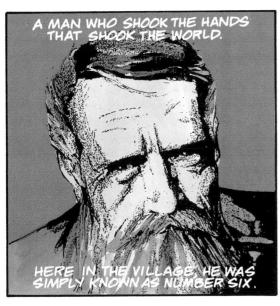

A MAN WHO SHOOK THE HANDS THAT SHOOK THE WORLD.

HERE IN THE VILLAGE, HE WAS SIMPLY KNOWN AS NUMBER SIX.

WHY DO YOU THINK NUMBER SIX IS STILL HERE?

WHY WOULDN'T HE BE HERE?

AND YOU'RE HERE...

book

Confrontation

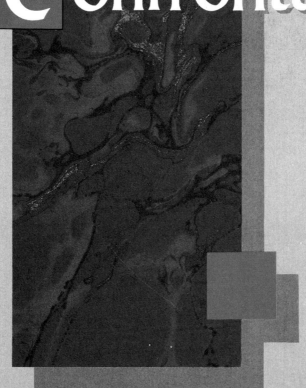

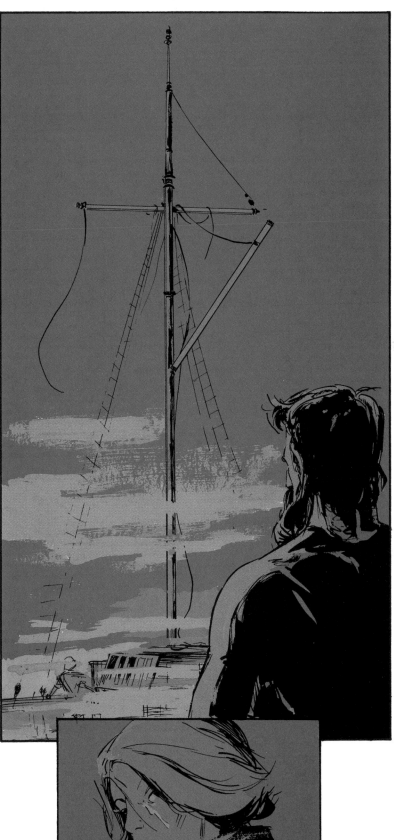

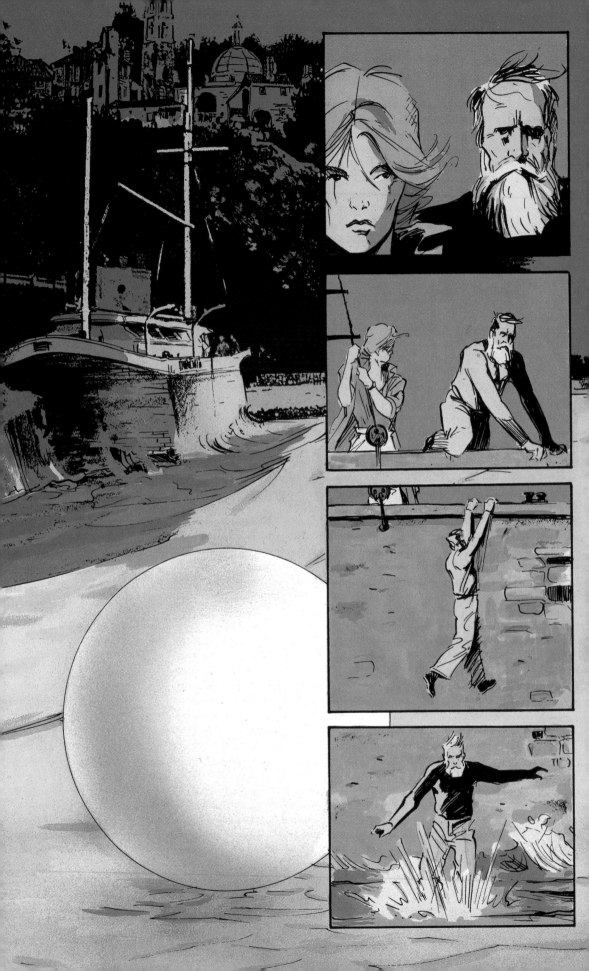

AH, THOMAS.

THANKS FOR DROPPING BY.

WELL, BARB FELT IT WAS TOP PRIORITY ON MY AGENDA.

THE AGENDA RULES.

ANYTHING TO DRINK?

JUST WATER, THANKS.

BESIDES, I WANTED TO ASK IF YOUR BOYS HAD SNOOPED THROUGH MY FLAT.

WHY?

WAS YOUR PLACE RANSACKED?

WE HAVE REASON TO BELIEVE THIS MAN IS A FOREIGN OPERATIVE. EVIDENCE SUGGESTS HE SABOTAGED THE NAVIGATION SYSTEM.

FURTHER...

WE SUSPECT HIM OF MURDER.

MURDER?

MY WIFE?

OH, NO. MARTIN LAKE, THE AGENT WHO WAS FOLLOWING YOU.

YOU ARE ATTENDING HIS FUNERAL THIS EVENING, AREN'T YOU?

MINISTRY SOLIDARITY.

YES... OF COURSE.

ONCE UPON A TIME, IN A MAGIC KINGDOM, THERE WAS A SPECIAL COURT WITH SPECIAL KNIGHTS WHO FOUGHT DRAGONS. SECRET DRAGONS.

ONE DAY ONE OF THE KNIGHTS GREW WEARY.

HE THREW HIS SHIELD, UNBUCKLED HIS ARMOUR AND CRIED "ENOUGH!" THE OTHER KNIGHTS WHISPERED TO EACH OTHER. "DID HE SEE SOMETHING IN THE LAND OF DRAGONS?" "DOES HE KNOW SOMETHING WE DON'T?" "PERHAPS HE BREATHED DRAGON FUMES AND BECAME A DRAGON."

SO IT CAME TO PASS THAT THE ERRANT KNIGHT WAS LOCKED IN A TOWER AND VISITED REGULARLY BY A COURTIER CALLED NUMBER TWO. AND WITH EVERY NEW VISIT NUMBER TWO GREW A NEW FACE, AND A NEW BODY.

MEAN TWOS. LEAN TWOS. "WE HAVE THE MEANS" TWOS. KEEN TWOS. CLEAN TWOS. "GOD SAVE THE QUEEN" TWOS.

EACH DIFFERENT. EACH THE SAME. TWO FACED.

AND DARKNESS CAME TO THE KINGDOM. CLOUDS OF SUSPICION SETTLED OVER THE LAND. AND THE DRAGONS WERE FOUND IN THE MOST UNLIKELY PLACES. HIDING IN BEDS.   IN CABINETS.   CURLED UP TIGHTLY IN PLACES HIGH AND LOW.

A TERRIBLE BATTLE WAS PITCHED. THE TRUE KNIGHTS, SHINING BRIGHTLY, THEIR STANDARDS HELD HIGH, WERE THE FIRST TO GO, AND SOON A PROCLAMATION WAS TRUMPETED OVER THE LAND:
     "THE WAR IS OVER-- WE HAVE PREVAILED. "

BUT WHO'S TO SAY WHO WON?

THE KNIGHTS?

OR THE DRAGONS?

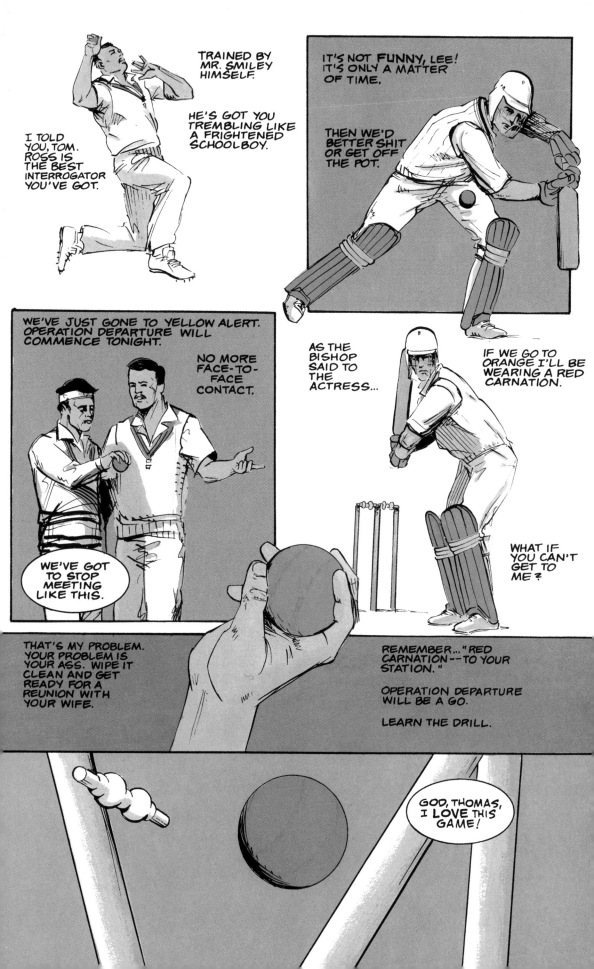

WHAT A PLEASANT COINCIDENCE BUMPING INTO YOU AGAIN, AFTER...

HOW LONG HAS IT BEEN?

NOT LONG ENOUGH.

WELL, YOUR *DRY* WIT HASN'T DESERTED YOU.

I KNEW YOU'D PLANT A SCOUT!

NOR YOU YOUR MINIONS.

BETTER YOUR ODDS!

TWO AGAINST ONE.

TWO?

DO YOU THINK I'M WITH HIM?

WARDER'S ATTITUDE...

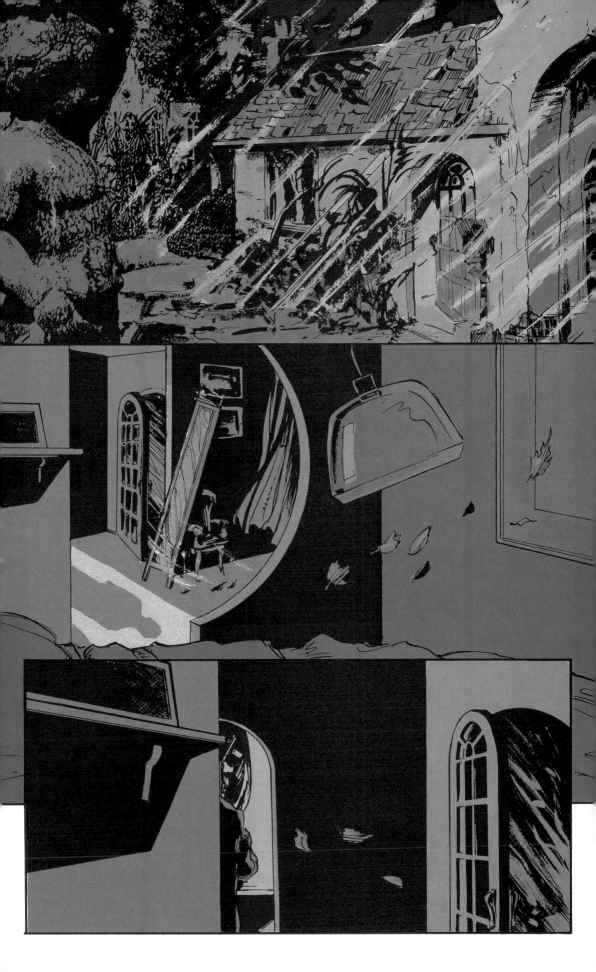

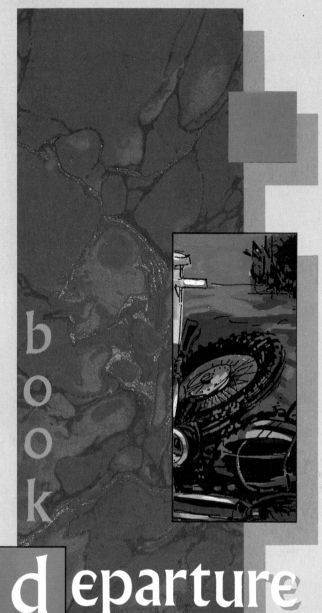

book **d**eparture

NOTHING ADDS UP. IT'S ALL SO TANTALIZINGLY ABSTRACT.

I FEEL CERTAIN THAT SOMETHING IS BEHIND SEVERAL RECENT EVENTS: MARTIN LAKE'S DEATH, PRESIDENT ZIA'S DEATH, THE VINCENNES ERROR. SOMETHING CALCULATED. A SINGLE INTELLIGENCE.

THAT'S WHY YOU'RE SUCH A GOOD D. OPS, ROSS. YOU HAVE THE RARE ABILITY TO FOCUS ON THE ESSENTIAL; AN EYE ON THE BIG PICTURE.

THANK YOU, SIR.

I JUST HOPE TO FIND THE LOOSE THREAD...

...AND PULL IT UNTIL EVERYTHING UNRAVELS.

COULD YOU BRING THE CAR AROUND PLEASE, HAYTHORNTHWAITE.

YES, SIR.

WHY WAS IT WRITTEN?

WELL, THE VILLAGE WAS A PROTOTYPE...

the village idiot

HAVEN'T YOU READ THE FILES?

YOUR PROTÉGÉ SEEMS TO HAVE DESTROYED THEM.

THOMAS? PISH-TOSH. HE'D NEVER DESTROY HIS FILES. AGAINST HIS NATURE. HE PROBABLY TUCKED THEM AWAY FOR SAFE-KEEPING.

ISN'T THOMAS COMING BY FOR TEA TODAY?

NO, HE CANCELLED THIS MORNING.

SOME URGENT BUSINESS.

I'LL TRY TO CATCH HIM AT THE OFFICE. THANK YOU, GEORGINA.

FEEL FREE TO DROP BY ANY TIME.

BE SEEING YOU.

SOUNDS LIKE WE'RE RAISING THE BLOODY TITANIC.
INDEED.
WHEN YOU'RE FINISHED, USE THE RECONNAISSANCE SIGNAL, AND WE'LL RETRIEVE YOU.
ANY QUESTIONS?
YES. WHEN DO WE LAND?
IMMEDIATELY.

I AM NOT A NUMBER!
I AM A FREE MAN!
I WILL NOT BE PUSHED, FILED, INDEXED, STAMPED, BRIEFED, DEBRIEFED, OR NUMBERED!
MY LIFE IS MY OWN!!
NUMBER SIX...
...IS DEAD!

ORBI ORBIT

LEE?

YOU WANTED TO KNOW THE HEART OF THE VILLAGE...

NOW YOU KNOW.

DID YOU FIND ANYTHING ON THE BEACH?

NOT MUCH. JUST SCARECROWS.

THIS WHOLE DROP HAS BEEN A BLOODY YAWNER.

NO SIGN OF HER BOAT?

VERY LITTLE. WE HAVE HER FLARE PISTOL. FOUND IT NEXT TO THIS STRANGE STUFF. NO IDEA WHAT IT IS.

THE BOYS AT THE LAB WILL LOVE IT.

THESE SCARECROWS ARE FILLED WITH EXPLOSIVES, TRIGGERED BY A SEISMOGRAPHIC SWITCH!

COR! IT'D TAKE AN EARTHQUAKE TO SET THAT OFF!

AT LEAST WE KNOW SOMEONE'S BEEN HERE!

KEEP SEARCHING.

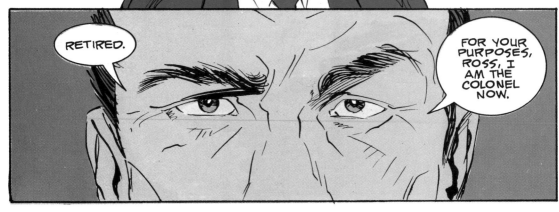

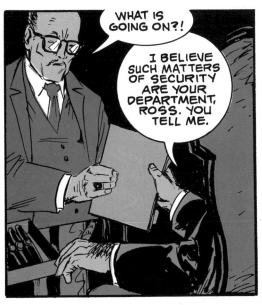

today...a beautiful day